D. FLORINE BAKER

GOD'S
ANGELS
WITH
SPECIAL
TALENTS

*God bless you!
D. Florine Baker
2007*

D. FLORINE BAKER

GOD'S
ANGELS
WITH
SPECIAL
TALENTS

ACW Press
Eugene, Oregon 97405

God's Angels with Special Talents
Copyright ©2004 D. Florine Baker
All rights reserved

Cover Design by Alpha Advertising
Interior design by Pine Hill Graphics

Packaged by ACW Press
85334 Lorane Hwy
Eugene, Oregon 97405
www.acwpress.com
The views expressed or implied in this work do not necessarily reflect those of ACW Press. Ultimate design, content, and editorial accuracy of this work is the responsibility of the author(s).

Publisher's Cataloging-in-Publication Data
(Provided by Cassidy Cataloguing Services, Inc.)

Baker, D. Florine.

   God's angels with special talents / D. Florine Baker. -- 1st ed. -- Eugene, OR. : ACW Press, 2004.

      p. ; cm.

      ISBN: 1-932124-32-2

      1. Baker, D. Florine. 2. Special education teachers--United States-- Biography. 3. Teachers--United States--Biography. I. Title.

LA2317.B343 B34 2004
371.9/092 [B]--dc22   0407

Printed in the United States of America.

This book is dedicated to the Lord, my Savior, Guide, and Protector of all the journeys of my life; to my daughter, who at age ten helped me on one of the trips for my students and another one while in college; to my son, who kept his father company while we were traveling; and to my wonderful husband, who always supported and allowed me to be gone for two weeks each year with my students. Also, to all who helped in any way for me to complete this story. May someone be encouraged to help a child in need along their way, with God's blessing.

$\mathcal{T}$rust in the Lord with all your
heart and lean not on your own
understanding; in all your ways
acknowledge Him, and He will
make your paths straight.

Proverbs 3:5-6

Foreword:
A Special Teacher

*C*hildren need, and deserve to have, caring adults in their lives. In many respects, it is a birthright. Parents have the most significant role in fulfilling this need. In an ideal situation, the parents are assisted by other relatives, a religious advisor, and competent and caring teachers.

When a child has the misfortune to be born into an environment where his parents refuse or are incapable of fulfilling their responsibilities, other adults have to step forward.

No one ever stepped forward quite like Florine Baker. Whether a child came from the best of homes or had no other significant adult in his life, he was indeed fortunate if he had Florine as his teacher.

I first met Florine when I was a young teacher. I continued to work with her as an assistant principal and later as a superintendent. I was amazed when I first came to realize what her brand of "hands on" education was really all about. Florine was a "hands on" teacher before any of us ever understood the term.

In all honesty, when I became a school super-intendent, my amazement was probably tempered somewhat by trepidation. I rested a bit uneasy when Florine headed off on her annual camping trip with a van filled with her students and their

$\mathscr{F}$lorine refers her students as "God's Angels with Special Talents," but *she* was really the one with the special talent.

provisions. No one was happier to see them return home safely.

I still enjoy having conversations with Florine's former students. For the most part, they are doing very well. Without exception, they give Florine credit for their success.

Florine refers her students as "God's Angels with Special Talents," but *she* was really the one with the special talent. She understood what each child was going through, and the special challenges in his life. She accepted each child where he was in life and gave him the personal and occupational skills needed to be successful in a challenging world. She taught him to care about himself and others. She made sure he knew someone cared about him. She refused to let him accept anything less than his very best, and she made sure his best was more than good enough.

No one ever experienced a teacher who gave her students more!

James L. Hartley,
Superintendent
Madison School District
Adrian, MI

Acknowledgments

I thank Julia Hanawalt for her direction, encouragement, and faith in me to complete this book. Without her guidance, it would never have been done. May God bless you, Julia. I also thank my dear friend Garnet Watters and her children, my brother Cloyce and Elaine Lidster, for housing our group on some of our trips. They gave us a place to pitch our tent, cook our food, and do our laundry. For them, we are grateful and blessed.

G ive her the reward she has
earned, and let her works bring
her praise at the city gate.
Proverbs 31:31

*F*or we are God's
workmanship, created in
Christ Jesus to do good works,
which God prepared in
advance for us to do.
Ephesians 2:10

It was He who gave some to be
apostles, some to be prophets,
some to be evangelists, and
some to be pastors and
teachers, to prepare God's
people for works of service,
so that the body of Christ may
be built up.
Ephesians 4:11,12

If our endeavors are successful, let's make sure we are thankful to God for His goodness, help, and protection.

Help me, O Lord, lest my heart becomes proud, for all of my talents by You are endowed; nothing I have can I claim as my own – what mercy and grace in my life You have shown!

Chapter One

*I*n the early 1930s, there were still one-room schools in southern Michigan. As a five-year-old in a country school in Ridgeway Township, Adrian, I was blessed with a fine, young teacher, Alice Hamilton, who taught me well. I took both kindergarten and first grade the same year.

I enjoyed school and played and learned with all the other children, but what stood out most for me was the discipline, tempered with kindness, displayed by Miss Hamilton. Once I was playing on the teeter-totter and got a sliver in my bottom.

$\mathcal{H}$er kindness and love dispelled the humiliation of the experience.

Miss Hamilton took me to the outtie and removed it. Her kindness and love dispelled the humiliation of the experience.

As she was in close contact with her pupils' parents, and had their total trust and support, she was able to maintain discipline. But she was sweet and young, so we naturally tested her. Once I defiantly went outside to the well for a drink, even though my parents had instructed me not to go outside in the rain without my boots on. I thought it would be okay because the well was just outside the door. Miss Hamilton spanked me. She taught me that there is no "partial" obedience to one's parents or teacher. She and I correspond to this day. I'm sure she had no idea I would become a teacher as well.

I turned eight years old the year my mother died of cancer, and my two younger siblings and I were cared for by a housekeeper. I became a real brat. Our pastor, Reverend Hawley, was a very kind, understanding person, and under his ministry, I understood Jesus' ways and gave my heart and life to Jesus. Pastor Hawley's daughter Naomi was a good friend, and we grew up together. She married my cousin, so now we're relatives.

I have been active in the church all my life and am so thankful that my parents took us to church every Sunday.

My family began every day with morning devotions. I have been active in the church all my life and am so thankful that my parents took us to church every Sunday and Wednesday and also to revival meetings. To me, the weeks just don't go well if I miss church. It is the Lord's Day, and I respect that.

My first stepmother, Dorothea, was a teacher and a strict disciplinarian, so I learned to do my housework, cook, and sew. The worst time was when she was my teacher in fourth grade. I was always accused of everything. One morning, she was reading to the class, and I was in the back when a piece of paper landed on my desk. She caught me with the note with the F word on it, so

I had done nothing wrong, and Dorothea and Dad both died never knowing the truth, as they surely didn't believe me.

I was spanked in front of the class. I was so embarrassed. Then at home that night, she told Dad, and he beat me with a strap. All of this, and I had done nothing wrong. I shall never forget that, and Dorothea and Dad both died never knowing the truth, as they surely didn't believe me.

Another time we had a hired farm hand to eat dinner with us, and I was told to pick a pan of spinach and wash it. Being a nine-year-old kid, I put it into a large dishpan and used my bare feet to sessile it up and down instead of washing it leaf by leaf. Well, needless to say, when it was cooked and on the table, it was very sandy. My punishment was to eat a large bowl of it, although no one else could. Yuck! I certainly didn't do that again, and to this day, spinach is not my favorite.

My Aunt Vadha was always like a mom to me and took me on trips and swimming at their cottage on the lake. She would buy me a dress when I didn't have anything but hand-me-downs. She

*J*n those days, girls had
two dresses for school,
one for Sundays, and some
everyday clothes.

was always special to me. In those days, girls had two dresses for school, one for Sundays, and some everyday clothes. I would wear one school dress one week and the other the next week. We always changed into our everyday clothes after school and after church to take care of them and make them last longer, as they had to be passed down in good condition to younger children. Today, girls can't decide what to wear and often change their clothes two or three times a day.

My Grandpa Lonnie was a very dear and patient man who had palsy. I had to help him most of the time since I was the oldest and Dorothea was too busy. I helped him walk and eat, and I catheterized him when he had to urinate. This I hated with a passion, but he was very kind and patient. Sometimes I would make him wait and wait, and now I feel bad about that even though I certainly would never make my daughter take on

_H_e was a small man, but could play the violin, and also could build anything from barns to churches, houses to furniture.

a task like that. It was really not a job for a young girl.

I was with him when he died at our home when I was eleven years old. Then Grandpa Cook, Dorothea's father, came to live with us, and he was a very special person. I heard him tell Dorothea she was too hard on me. He was a small man, but could play the violin, and also could build anything from barns to churches, houses to furniture. He had even made a violin for Dorothea when she graduated from high school. When I graduated, he made me a beautiful cedar chest with strips of light

*G*randpa was always encouraging me and loved me very much.

and dark wood for the cover. I cherish it to this day. When Don and I married, he gave me a chest of drawers to match the cedar chest, and I'm still using it also.

Grandpa was always encouraging me and loved me very much. His daughter, Kay, was my very favorite aunt and her husband, Dewey, my favorite uncle. At our wedding reception, they gave my husband a key to their lodge and said that we could stay as long as we liked. The lodge was on a parcel of land larger than three hundred acres that included five lakes. They welcomed us to use their place for youth group weekends and vacations many times until it was sold last year. Aunt Kay was like a mom to me and I miss her very much. We named our son after Uncle Dewey and our daughter after Aunt Kay, so we still have a Dewey and Miala Kay.

As I grew up, I was active in the 4-H group and learned many things that coincided with life on a farm. The first year, I learned to darn socks, hem a dishtowel, and make a basic skirt. Once, in school, we showed some of the items we had worked on, and the teacher said, in front of everyone, that I couldn't have darned that sock so well myself; someone else must have done it. Being called a liar didn't set well with me, so I told my stepmother, who came to school the next morning to assure the teacher that I had done the work myself.

That same teacher tried to teach us how to make clothes. At the time, the only dresses I had were hand-me-downs from my aunts. I had no practice in completing an entire garment, and the teacher did not guide me well, so my stepmother took the dress apart and remade it so that it was fit to be worn. As a young girl of nine, I did learn to sew and continued sewing the rest of my life, making most of my clothes as well as clothes for my family.

Chapter Two

When I was still quite young, I found I was good in art and also in writing poems, and I have always been good at anything I could make with my hands. I designed the cover of our class history booklet and wrote several poems that were in it. I also took summer classes in watercolors and in oils and enjoy painting every chance I get. My latest was painting on fungus. A friend, Mr. Revard, found a twelve- by eighteen-inch fungus and asked me to paint a picture of his cabin on it. He was very happy when he saw it and still brags to everyone.

You will always find me busy with gardening in the spring. We plant peas, and usually get at least three to five gallons to pod, eat, and freeze. We have green onions, beets, beans, cabbage, and lots

*O*n our farm, we were very busy. Although my husband, Don, worked for Uncle Sam at the post office, we also farmed two hundred acres.

of sweet corn and tomatoes. I freeze and can until my shelves and freezer are full. Canning pickles and relish is also great fun. I enjoy giving my family and friends jars of jam from the red raspberries and thimbleberries we pick.

On our farm, we were very busy. Although my husband, Don, worked for Uncle Sam at the post office, we also farmed two hundred acres. We had chickens, pigs, sheep, and cows. I took care of the chores very often, especially in the summer. I also drove the tractor and held Dewey on my lap to fit the fields for planting. I worked in the garden, mowed the lawn, and took care of the flowers. I canned lots of vegetables and fruits: peaches, pears, and plums. I also canned tomatoes and string beans and made relish and pickles.

Of course I had learned to sew as a young girl of nine, as I have mentioned, and made most of our clothes for myself as well as for my family. I made my wedding gown, five bridesmaid gowns, and two flower-girl dresses, as well as aprons for the cooks and little waitresses at our reception.

Cooking is another of my hobbies. I've been cooking all my life. I joined a mission trip to St. Lucia, an island in the Caribbean once and cooked three meals a day for two weeks for thirty

I've made many cakes for
special occasions, such as
graduations, baby showers,
birthdays, and other weddings.

adults. What a grand experience. The cake decorating class I took was also great fun. I made our son Dewey's wedding cake and our daughter

Miala's as well. They were both so tall I had to stand on a chair to decorate the tops. I've also made many other cakes for special occasions, such as graduations, baby showers, birthdays, and other weddings.

I have knitted a few items, but crocheting is what I really enjoy. I've made over twenty doilies as

*E*verywhere I go, I look for a student so that I can pass on what I learn.

gifts this past year alone. I'm also making quilts for my grandchildren as they graduate from high school. I have two done and two more to go. When I asked my grandson Josh what pattern he wanted for his quilt, he said, "It doesn't matter, Grandma, as long as it's blue." That made my day.

This past winter I learned to paint on glass with a group of lady friends while we were visiting in South Texas. I will now teach others to do the same. Everywhere I go, I look for a student so that I can pass on what I learn.

30

Information and skills are never really new; there are just many people who don't know these things yet, and always providing an opportunity for "each one to teach one."

Chapter Three

I believe that God gives life and also takes life. My parents made a mistake and I was on the way before they were married. I'm so thankful they did not abort me before they were married, even though back then, in 1928, they were ostracized and looked down upon. I was loved and well taken care of, and I didn't know about this until I was a teenager. It was a big shock to me, as it made me wonder if they really wanted me or if they had married because of me. I really never found out that answer, but God has been faithful and led me all these years.

I graduated from high school in 1945 at the end of World War II. There was a great shortage of teachers, as many had gone to war. My stepmother heard about a school called the Lenawee Monroe County Normal School and thought it would be good for me. Being a shy farm girl, I wasn't sure.

$\mathcal{W}$e learned how to plan lessons for all the grades and how to evaluate the students' work.

We checked it out and I enrolled in September. Our class of twenty-three girls and one fellow was taught by one teacher the first semester. These students and I all became very close and have been close now for over fifty years.

The books we learned from in class contained all the information we would be teaching in the fall of 1946. In the first semester, all the different subjects were thoroughly covered, so we knew everything we were to teach the children. We learned how to plan lessons for all the grades and how to evaluate the students' work. For such a

short period of time, the training was very thor-
ough. We even learned to identify by sight fifty

$\mathscr{I}$ love people of all ages, especially anyone with a need or problem.

birds found in Michigan. This has been valuable
to me ever since, in both my teaching and in my
personal enjoyment.

The second semester we all went to different
schools and did our practice teaching under the
supervision of other teachers. I sure enjoyed working with children. I love people of all ages, especially anyone with a need or problem. My special
love has been working with teenagers. They are
such a challenge and a joy. Occasionally they are a
disappointment, but more often a blessing.

Before I started teaching, I worked in the summer for a cousin taking care of three children.
Grandma Hawley had an old 1934 Ford coupe
which I bought with $300 I had saved. I painted it
blue. It was sure a lot of fun to drive, and my
friends called it the Blue Goose. Money was so

tight that I tried to use only one tank of gasoline each week. Often, if I ran out of gas on Friday after school, I would call my cousin Harold, who would

$\mathscr{A}$t nineteen, I started teaching in a one-room school.

say in a resigned voice, "Where are you this time?" He would bring a can of gas and off I'd go. He is still a special cousin. I only wish I hadn't sold the Blue Goose, as I would love to go for a ride in it now.

At nineteen, I started teaching in a one-room school called Barrett School. It was about four miles from the little town of Britton, Michigan, on a country road near a farmhouse. I enjoyed teaching the twenty-eight students in grades K through 8. We were given a new U.S. flag, so we had a ceremony to burn the old flag. We built a bonfire and put a large rock in the center. We pledged the old flag and took it down, carefully making sure it never touched the ground. Two of the oldest boys took it to the fire and held the flag over it, letting it burn, then dropping the last bit onto the rock to finish burning. We then surrounded the flagpole and as the boys raised the new, beautiful flag, we pledged it and sang "The Star Spangled Banner." Each student felt very proud to be an American and proud of our flag. It was a good experience, learning to respect our flag, our government, and our country. I'm still interested in our country and the policies our government officials make for us to live by. I receive a variety of mail concerning different groups that are trying to keep America free, moral, and an example to other countries around the world.

I was asked if I drank alcohol or smoked, as they didn't want a teacher who did.

Our school was run by a school board made up of a director, a treasurer, and a secretary. These men were farmers in the district whose children were students in the school. They interviewed me for my job and were very kind. I was asked if I drank alcohol or smoked, as they didn't want a teacher who did. It was important to the school board and especially to the parents that the teacher in charge of their children have the same value system as the families in the district. In this case, they were church-going farm families. They wanted someone with the same moral and ethical

$\mathscr{A}$ teacher must have upright values and a moral lifestyle in order to be a positive influence on the children in her care.

base as they, someone who was prepared to teach what farm children needed to know.

A teacher must have upright values and a moral lifestyle in order to be a positive influence on the children in her care, so that they can become a positive influence in turn. These children's parents expected them to grow up, become responsible adults, and have families as they, themselves, did. The children grew up with these expectations. Whatever they do in life, they are ultimately ambassadors of our country; policies regarding education need to reflect strong moral values to produce responsible, moral citizens.

I made plans to be the best teacher I could be. As the oldest of five siblings, I wanted to set a good example. I also wanted my parents to be proud of me. I studied hard and found ways to teach the subjects so the students would be interested in them. I naturally love children and know that they need hugs. When I worked with younger students, I would often set one on my lap while teaching. The students wanted to be like the teacher, wear their hair like the teacher, and get hugs from the teacher. These children would grow up to be parents, educators, and farmers, and would probably always have contact in some way with children. What better time to teach them how to show love and affection?

The last day of my first year of teaching, I came home and found my stepmother in great pain. She was taken to the hospital and died that week with a blood clot shutting off the circulation to her legs. This was a very difficult time. At age eight, I had lost my own mother to cancer; now the only one I really knew as mom was also gone. I was left with the full responsibility of the four younger ones. The youngest was only two years old. I canned over one hunderd jars of garden produce that summer, besides cleaning, cooking, laundry, and garden work.

A picture of my students in the country school, 1954.

Chapter Four

I taught at the Barrett School for three years until it was consolidated into the Britton School District. I then was hired by the Britton district the next year to teach a combination room of fifth and sixth graders. We had a principal from Norway whose daughter was in my fifth grade class. She was a perfect student with beautiful long blonde braids. Her name was Miala, and I liked the name so much that when our daughter was born, we named her Miala Kay.

In 1947, children walked or rode their bikes to school together as a group. Some came from the north, others from the south. Some walked two or more miles each way to school and home again. It was good exercise and fun at the same time. It was a happy group, and everyone looked out for each other.

If students caused any problems at school, or didn't get their work done and had to stay after

I taught whatever I knew to whoever was willing to learn.

school, they would be walking alone later and everyone knew they were in trouble. It was very seldom that we had trouble; first of all, if the older children did anything naughty, they knew the younger kids would tattle. And second, if a student didn't understand his lessons, there was always another student who would help. The children were there to learn. Two girls from one family wanted to learn to play the piano, so since we had one at school, I gave them lessons two days each week at lunch time, and they did learn to play. I taught whatever I knew to whoever was willing to learn.

The families in the district were farmers and were honest, clean, and honorable people. They attended church on Sunday and expected their children to do the same. I had only one unsettling incident. Once when I was working late after school, a father came in and asked me to figure how much his round freezer would hold. He gave me the radius dimensions, and as I was busy figuring it out, I found his arm around me. I jumped up and said, "You get out now, and never come back here without your wife." After that, I kept the door locked when I was there alone. I was just a

*C*hildren then didn't want
as many things as children
do today. They were satisfied
with clean clothes; warm
coats, hats and gloves; and
paper, pencils and pens.

green young schoolteacher, and he had the wrong idea that he could get away with anything with me. I never had any trouble after that, either with students or their parents.

43

Children then didn't want as many things as children do today. They were satisfied with clean clothes; warm coats, hats and gloves; and paper, pencils and pens. They didn't have to have large fancy gyms in schools; the children walked or rode their bikes to school for exercise and played ball at recess. I was usually pitcher for both teams as running bases wasn't my long shot. Most children learn best by doing things actively or hands-on learning, and if they are kept busy, they're happy and they aren't missing anything.

They carried their lunches, but during the winter months, I sometimes made hot chocolate and

I believe you must love
children and love God to be
able to lead and teach them
how to live and learn.

they would often bring potatoes, which we baked in the big heating stove in the center of the room. That hit the spot on cold days. A pot of chili, goulash, or soup was sometimes furnished by a family. School days were long, and the moms understood the need for a hot meal on those cold, Michigan winter days.

I truly loved those good old school days. I believe you must love children and love God to be

A teacher must be moral,
honest, and loving. Children
love to be hugged and praised,
and to be encouraged to be the
very best they can be.

able to lead and teach them how to live and learn. A teacher must be moral, honest, and loving. Children love to be hugged and praised, and to be encouraged to be the very best they can be.

We started every day with the pledge to Old Glory and the Lord's Prayer. Each morning of the school week, I would read a chapter of a good book like *Heidi*. We had music one morning; a Bible story one morning; sharing time one morning, and job assignments one morning. Everyone enjoyed this time.

We had no special-needs children, as with nine years of repetitive instruction and recitation, they were bound to get, at some point, what they may have missed earlier. If a student was absent or sick and didn't understand something one day, he or

*T*here is a big difference between understanding concepts and being able to break a concept down and teach it to a group of students.

she certainly figured it out after hearing the material taught to each grade for those nine years. They all learned how to read well and do math and all the other subjects. In a one-room school, there was plenty of opportunity for me to individualize the teaching to different interests and ability levels. It was the best educational system we ever had. Each child received individual attention and love, so they were well-adjusted young people who became well-adjusted adults.

There is a big difference between understanding concepts and being able to break a concept down and teach it to a group of students whose comprehension levels are varied. The ability to teach in this manner requires intuition, perception, stamina, and gifts from God. I believe you have to teach the whole child. Students who are always in a class with other students their own age may not get the same well-rounded education these kids received in the country school because much more of their time is spent on the educational concepts and not intermingling between age levels. They don't see what is being learned at the

**𝒟iscipline is very important
as long as it is based on the
character, morality, and
spiritual training of the
Ten Commandments.**

different levels, both educationally and socially. The country-school kids saw older kids being kind to younger ones; all were taught to respect their elders and to be nice to younger children.

Discipline is very important as long as it is based on the character, morality, and spiritual training of the Ten Commandments. Without this, we have disrespect, disobedience, and the awful chaos in most public schools today. The best educational program ever was the country school. It was small enough to give individual attention to each student.

The adventure of teaching has been exactly where God planned for me to be, of that I'm sure.

A teacher has a lot of responsibility when she has twenty-three young minds and hearts in her care for at least 285 days a year, seven hours a day.

I taught kindergarten through the eighth grade. It was a big job to teach all the subjects to all the grades, but I surely did enjoy it. A teacher has a lot of responsibility when she has twenty-three young minds and hearts in her care for at least 285 days a year, seven hours a day.

Christmas was a wonderful time when we celebrated the birthday of Jesus. Our Christmas programs were a real production and everyone in the district, parents and friends, would pack the school. A fellow in the district would be Santa and bring his bag of gifts at the end of the program. We took boxes and made floodlights, and I put

$\mathscr{O}$ne spring, it rained very hard; the road became impossible to drive on.

chalk drawings on the blackboard for scenery. The older students helped the younger ones, and I would sit out front and play the piano when needed. It was always very quiet backstage and the children did a great job. The school was always packed and everyone enjoyed it.

The year brought all kinds of challenges. One spring, it rained very hard; the road became impossible to drive on and even too muddy for the children to walk on. So the board members fixed a trailer with board seats and a canvas over the top. Each morning for a week, I left my Blue Goose at one of the board members' house on the black-top, and the children and I rode to school in the trailer pulled by a John Deere tractor. Then they picked us up after school for the return trip. What friends we all became. Six of these little girls were waitresses at my wedding. They thought riding on that trailer was the greatest fun. These children were always respectful and obeyed all the rules. One of the young fellows, Kenny Bortel, still calls me "Teach" whenever he sees me.

You see, when the parents came the first day of school with their children, they would say, "Now you be good and mind the teacher or she will spank you, and when you get home, I will spank you again." You can be sure we had no problems. Also, the older students would help the younger ones, so we had not one failing. I know this is the best and most rewarding job in the world, helping young people become successful in life.

Chapter Five

I started teaching Sunday school as a young teenager and taught one group or another for over fifty years. I was youth director and Sunday school teacher all the years my children were teenagers. I have been active in the church all my life and am so thankful that my parents took us every Sunday and Wednesday, and to revival meetings. My family began every day with morning devotions. To me, the weeks just don't go well if I miss church. It is the Lord's Day and I respect that.

There are many activities that churches can arrange to keep the young people busy. We took canoe trips and sometimes we had seventy-five young people to feed and look after on a weekend. We had graduation banquets each year. We took them to the beach on Sunday afternoons to witness and report back at the Sunday night youth

*E*ach summer I would drive a vanload of teens from our church to Camp Caesar in West Virginia where they had great fun and spiritual lessons.

meetings. At Christmas, seventy-five to a hundred went caroling, ending up at our home for homemade lasagna, potato salad, homemade rolls, and dessert. We had hayrides and pond parties. Then each summer I would drive a vanload of teens from our church to Camp Caesar in West Virginia where they had great fun and spiritual lessons each day in the company of young Christians from other states.

I was always camp counselor to a cabin of girls, which was such a blessing. The girls from the South were always so cute. They would call me

"Mama B" in their Southern drawl. Our son met his wife Vicki at church camp, and what a blessing she has been to our family. People would ask how I could take time to go to camp every year. To me, it was the greatest thing I could do for my young people. Two of them married and now have a son studying to be a minister. One of my students, Tom Dinius, was saved on one of our trips and realized that he should devote his life to the Lord. He is now married to a nurse and is on the mission

I taught about God and His love for everyone and the joy of serving Him all the days of our lives so that we will live with Him for all eternity.

field. It pays to serve God and be a true witness for Him. Tom invited me to his ordination and had me stand while he told how I was responsible for him serving the Lord today. I have truly been blessed to have been a teacher.

I love to study for my classes. Whether in school or Sunday school, I taught about God and

His love for everyone and the joy of serving Him all the days of our lives so that we will live with Him for all eternity. What better goal can one have? For many years, I had the privilege to have a Bible club in school. I had a good group of young people,

*T*hat was when we could pray in school, read the Bible, and have the Ten Commandments on the wall.

and we were responsible for the Thanksgiving, Christmas, and Easter programs in school assemblies. It was a great opportunity. Ministers gave a talk of encouragement to the students. We also had skits and other programs, and all enjoyed them. That was when we could pray in school, read the Bible, and have the Ten Commandments on the wall along with the pictures of George Washington and Abe Lincoln. Today, I wonder how many students would know who they are. We never had the disrespect, disobedience, and shootings then. The Bible tells us we are to train up the children in the way of the Lord, and when they are old, they will not depart from it. I found that so true in my family and the families of my friends. But we must teach precept on precept and set an example for them to follow.

Chapter Six

One of the greatest challenges in my teaching career took place when I was teaching fifth grade with three other teachers. One teacher taught math, one taught English, and one taught history. I taught science to 120 students. We each had thirty homeroom students. When the year began, the students all came in saying, "I hate science." I made it my goal right then that they would love science by the year's end. We started out studying the planets and we divided into groups. Each group chose the planet they wanted to learn about. They researched and then we used wire and papier-maché for the planets and painted them. We hung them from the ceiling

_L_earning about science included health and safety, and was taught in different environments than just the classroom.

spaced out the way they are in the solar system. The children were learning and having a ball.

Learning about science included health and safety, and was taught in different environments than just the classroom. We planned a hayride at one student's home and made a bonfire, followed by a hot dog and marshmallow roast. This was the kind of learning that really got their attention.

Then Christmas was coming and we had one or two students from each group who were paper-boys. We talked about what we could do for someone for Christmas. We found lonely people on the paper routes and began to learn a couple of carols to sing when we delivered our packages to them. I had a stove and oven in my classroom, so the children made cookie dough at home, brought it to class, and we baked cookies. We also made fudge and packed eight shoeboxes. Then we wrapped them. We planned the route we would take, and during the two days before Christmas break, we walked to the homes, sang, and delivered our boxes and wished them a very happy

*S*ome of the people were so happy and pleased they cried; some of the children cried also.

Christmas. Some of the people were so happy and pleased they cried; some of the children cried also. We discussed the project later and talked about how they learned science through cooking, and learned sharing through science. They all said it was the nicest thing they had ever done—to see people so happy.

Then in January, we started the study of plants, learning many wildflowers by name and their parts and purposes. We grew lima beans and castor beans from seeds. By planting the seed in a glass jar with the seed to the outside of a wet paper napkin, we could watch the roots grow and then watch as it opened and grew out at the top. The first thing the students did each day was to run to the glass jars to see what was new.

Next we found that some students had chickens, so I bought an incubator and we put the eggs in and watched the temperature closely, turning the eggs until we had a few chicks pecking out of the shell. What excitement this was.

In May, the whole group traveled by bus, with suitcases, to a wildlife camp for a week. The stu-

The students had their classes outdoors. The teachers set up challenging lessons for the different curriculums.

dents had their classes outdoors. The teachers set up challenging lessons for the different curriculums. For instance, the math class measured an area equal to an acre. In science, we took nature hikes and learned about different trees and leaves so the students could identify them. We also collected and pressed leaves, and made scrapbooks.

A biologist came with our group to teach us about a bog and bog life. We walked out on a bog, which

*E*ach morning we started
with the pledge to the flag,
the Lord's Prayer, and sang
"The Star Spangled Banner."

fascinated us all, as we were standing on roots floating on water.

We ate our meals, played games, and learned together. This camp experience was looked forward to each year. Now, all the children liked science as their favorite class, and I was really happy about that. So to finish out the year, I invited one of the groups and their parents to our farm on each of the last four Saturdays of the school year for a picnic and fun. One of the parents came to me and said that his appreciation of a teacher had been renewed to think I put so much extra time into teaching the children. This was a compliment that surely made me want to do even better next year.

In my homeroom, I had a piano, so each morning we started with the pledge to the flag, the

Lord's Prayer, and sang "The Star Spangled Banner." I had so many parents tell me how much they appreciated the way I taught their children. I

I **never ever had one parent in over the thirty-two years of teaching ever complain about the Lord's Prayer.**

never ever had one parent in the hundreds of students, over the thirty-two years of teaching, ever complain about the Lord's Prayer or anything else. One of my friends, who was a missionary and contractor in Africa, had a large collection of slides and animal skins he had brought back with him. He brought these to my class, and the students were thrilled to see and feel them. The principal even came to sit in on the class and enjoyed it very much.

Near the end of that second year of teaching in the same school system with the same teachers, I went to see the principal at lunch time one noon, and he told me he had nothing but good to say about my teaching and was going to recommend to the board that I be tenured. I was pleased and went back to eat lunch with the other teachers, who wanted to know why I was late. I told them what he said. It wasn't long before I found one of the teachers listening at my open door and the principal began asking about the morning prayer. The older teachers I worked with became downright unfriendly, and I decided rather than continue to teach in this environment, I would resign.

$\mathcal{I}$ began packing up to leave, not knowing where I was going the next year, but I felt content as I knew God was in charge.

The parents with other children entering fifth grade the next year were very upset. I had just earned my bachelor's degree and was happy in my job until this came up. Then one day, the principal asked if I was staying, and I decided I could not stay. I began packing up to leave, not knowing where I was going the next year, but I felt content as I knew God was in charge.

The day I left, I asked the principal what the real problem had been, and he said he could answer that in one word: *jealousy*. I told him, "That was your problem and you should have

$\mathscr{I}$ was offered a job teaching special students (special education) at twice the previous salary.

taken care of it." To this day, he can't look me in the eye. My husband was shocked that I had quit, but I told him, "Don't worry, God will provide." So we went on vacation and when we returned just a week before school was to start, I received a call telling me there was an opening at Madison School in Adrian, Michigan. I made an appointment for an interview the next day. I was offered a job teaching special students (special education) at twice the previous salary, taken to lunch, and given a tour of our district. I felt like a queen for a day. Of course, I signed the contract even though I did not have a certificate yet to teach special education.

Later, back at home, I told my family to sit down as they wouldn't believe how God had worked it all out. God is so good. He had prepared me all my previous years in the country school teaching kindergarten through eighth grades to teach these special students. I loved working with these students for the next twenty-two years. I feel that when one takes a stand for what is right, God always blesses.

A great joy took place seven years later when a mother of one of my Onsted students called me and invited me to her son's graduation open house. The class had voted me their favorite teacher of all their school years and they wanted me to come and see them all again. We had a great time talking about the many good times we had in fifth grade. God never fails us when we trust and obey Him.

Chapter Seven

Since there was only one fellow in our County Normal teacher's training, we girls found dates in other places. I started dating a fellow at church. We had known each other since we were kids, and I used to get angry with him because he would pull my pigtails and look so innocent. But in our late teens, I started liking him. He was a farm boy and I a farm girl. After graduation, he took agricultural classes at East Lansing, and I went to County Normal to become a teacher.

Don finally asked me to go with him to a Sunday school class party one muddy spring evening in March, and I said I would. He then asked if our roads were good, and I said they were, but he barely got through as the mud was up to the running boards. He wrote from school and we continued to date for the next four years.

*W*hen we came home, we found our apartment had been truly messed up as a joke.

In a beautiful church wedding, August 1, 1950, Don and I were married by his Uncle George, who was a Nazarene preacher. We set up housekeeping after we returned from our honeymoon, where we spent some time in the Upper Peninsula of Michigan and also stayed at our Aunt Kay and Uncle Dewey's beautiful cabin on five lakes in White Cloud in the Lower Peninsula. We had a wonderful time. When we came home, we found our apartment had been truly messed up as a joke. Our landlords, Mom and Pop Hall, were wonderful people who became our dear friends.

Don enlisted in the army and served in Germany as an M.P. for Uncle Sam. I sailed over on the *U.S. America*, a beautiful ship, and had a great ten-day trip on board with friends. It was a great adventure for me. I found that another girl in my area was going to France to be with her husband, so we went together. She disembarked in Le Havre, and I sailed on to Bremerhaven, where I was so glad to see my husband waiting for me. He had found a large one-room apartment in the home of Hatta and her husband Hans, who had been one of Hitler's bodyguards during the war.

*H*e brought me back a black boot with a rat on the toe as a gift from his mother.

His job now was a steward on a German ship. We became very close friends. In fact since they had no children, Hans called me his daughter, *meine Tochter*, in German. They did not have a car, and when his mother died in Breman, we let him borrow our car for a three-day trip. He brought me back a black boot with a rat on the toe as a gift from his mother. It was to remind me of the story of the pied piper and the rats he led out of town.

We enjoyed our time overseas. Once we took Hans and Hatta on a picnic, spread out our blanket and ate our lunch. Then we rented paddle

*W*hen Christmas came, we celebrated it together in German style.

bikes and paddled around the nearby lake. When Christmas came, we celebrated it together in German style. On Christmas Eve, Hatta made German potato salad and fried carp for our meal. It was very different but delicious. The Christmas tree was in the hall. The kitchen, our room, and their room all had doors leading into the hall, and we shared the kitchen. We had such fun on Christmas Eve, decorating the tree all in silver and white lights. While putting on the icicles, Hans hung them in clumps, and I said, "*Eins* by *eins*." He had a good laugh at that, as I was learning German, and was telling him "one by one."

On Christmas Day, we gave them American-type gifts, and they gave us German-type gifts. I still have the *popo* wash cloths with *Fater* and *Muter* on the mitten-shaped cloths. Very handy for the purpose of washing private areas.

Hans and Hatta took us to visit her brother's family on his farm. We enjoyed meeting Opah and Omah, the grandparents. The German farm homes are connected to the barn, and we were entertained in the living room, which was only

*𝒯*he Christmas tree was lit by small candles, and how they kept them from catching the tree on fire, I don't know.

used for company or special days. The Christmas tree was lit by small candles, and how they kept them from catching the tree on fire, I don't know. They took us into the barn part of the house, where a mother pig lived with her family of ten piglets. We then went with Opah to another shed where the cow was kept and saw how they chopped beets to feed it. The large oven for baking bread was also outside. We went several times to visit them on the farm and always took popcorn for Opah. He had never had any until then (1955), and he enjoyed it a lot. We enjoyed being with them even though they knew very little English and I spoke very poor German.

The last time we visited them before we came home, they gave us their spinning wheel, which

*T*heir custom was to give
something of theirs to us that
they knew we would like.

they had used during the Second World War era. Their custom was to give something of theirs to us that they knew we would like. I still have the spinning wheel and enjoy it today. They were a wonderful German couple.

Hatta also introduced us to an elderly couple who lived upstairs in our apartment house, Herr and Frau Bretchnieder. They had no children and were very poor, but lovely, loving people. I often went to visit them and took them cookies and candies, which they enjoyed very much. Herr Bretchnieder died and we went to pay respects at the mausoleum, as they had no money for more. He was laid out with a white night shirt, no teeth, and in a very small space with a sheet over his lower half. Individual flowers were placed on the sheet. Candles were lit, but there was no heat, and this was a very cold November.

Then Hatta said I had to dress in black to go to the funeral. This I did, and taking a handful of flowers, we walked to the mausoleum where a blind man played the organ. I couldn't understand any of the service. Everyone was dressed in black and the pallbearers wore black boat-style hats and carried the casket through the cemetery to the burial spot. We all followed behind and

*W*e bowed a few seconds and threw in our flowers and three scoops of dirt. This was a hard task for me.

stood in the snow while each person went up to the burial spot where an urn of soil with a scoop stood. We bowed a few seconds and threw in our flowers and three scoops of dirt. This was a hard task for me, but Frau Bretschnieder was very grateful. She asked me to spend the afternoon with her and her neighbors and friends remembering her husband.

The next day she asked me to walk with her to the grave, as she did for several days to honor her

I found people to translate her German for me, and she found someone to translate for her.

beloved husband. Later I wrote to her, but as I understood very little German, I wrote in English. I found people to translate her German for me, and she found someone to translate for her. She was a very nice lady and friend to us. When she passed away, she had asked her lawyer to write and let us know, which he did. In all our travels, we found that if you are a friend to others, they will be your friend. We make friends everywhere we go. God is so good.

We found the German people very friendly, hard working, and happy. All in all, we traveled to thirteen countries during our stay in Europe.

I have many girlfriends, but the best, for over forty-five years, is my dear friend Garnet. We met in

Germany while our husbands were in the service. She and I always enjoyed going to the market to get fresh fruit and vegetables each week. One day, Garnet's car stalled on the trolley tracks, and the trolley driver was ding, ding, dinging his bell. I started giggling, and poor Garnet couldn't get the

*T*he fellows in the trolley
jumped off and pushed us off
the tracks. We get a good laugh
over that to this day.

car started. Finally, the fellows in the trolley jumped off and pushed us off the tracks. We get a good laugh over that to this day. The trolley fellows were very nice and had compassion for us when they realized we were both very much in the family way. We each had our first child there, just six weeks apart. We really couldn't be closer. We shopped together, exercised together, cried and laughed together, and truly enjoyed each other's company. We sometimes talk to each other on the phone several times a day even though she lives in Tennessee and I live in Michigan. We also get together as often as possible. We are always there for each other. I've had and still have so many wonderful friends; God has blessed me abundantly.

Our beautiful son, Dewey, was born on September 2, 1956, in Bremerhaven at the U.S. hospital. He was such a happy baby and we were very proud parents. His daddy was always tossing him in the air and catching him, and he would giggle for more. Three months later, we sailed home on the navy ship, the *Upsure*, just before

$\mathcal{O}$ur ship rocked so badly that Don's shoes would slide from wall to wall in our stateroom.

Christmas. Since Dewey was so young, Donald was allowed to stay with us and not down in the hold with the other army recruits. We ran into very rough seas and had waves thirty-five feet high. Many of the troops were sick, as were some of the crew members. Don was also sick. Our ship rocked so badly that Don's shoes would slide from wall to wall in our stateroom. Baby Dewey very happily rocked in his bunk, though. I went to take a bath and the water nearly sloshed out of the tub. You had to put your hands out and catch yourself as you walked. One night, I went to the dining room to eat and was the only one there.

*T*he storm was so bad the captain had to stay on the bridge and keep the ship pointed into the wind so we would not capsize.

The waiter came and said, "You are right to come and eat," but he suddenly turned green and ran off to be sick. I then went back to the cabin. The ship's newspaper made the statement that the up-chuck bags everyone was carrying around should be red or green as those Christmas colors were very popular.

The storm was so bad the captain had to stay on the bridge and keep the ship pointed into the wind so we would not capsize. We received an SOS from another ship, but couldn't help. Water was coming over the lower decks and no one was allowed anywhere but the enclosed deck.

After the illness and danger, and after being gone for a year and a half from family and friends, it was a thrill to sail into New York harbor and view the beautiful lady, the Statue of Liberty. That sight brought tears to my eyes. We were home in America, the "good ol' USA."

Chapter Eight

*B*ack home, we busied ourselves with farm life. When Dewey was big enough, he was a good helper. I also took care of our fifteen-room house, taught Sunday school, and did substitute teaching in public school. I then decided to take some classes to get my BA degree from Adrian College. It was very hard to work this in, but I finally achieved it. Then our lovely daughter, Miala, was born, so I was really busy. God blessed us with a healthy little girl and we were very happy.

In 1964, Miala started school and I went back to get credits for my master's degree. In 1965, I returned to teaching full time. That's when I taught the fifth grade science in Onsted. We discussed this as a family, and the children said they

*W*e all worked together and then each summer we went to our cabin on Winslow Lake for our vacation in August.

would help more so that I could teach. We all worked together and then each summer we went to our cabin on Winslow Lake for our vacation in August when the farm could be left for two or three weeks at a time. We always had a neighbor friend to feed the animals. This was such a bonding family time. I was always home when the children were, as this was very important to me.

We celebrated fifty years of marriage in 2000, and Uncle George was there to congratulate us. God has blessed us with over fifty years together now and has given us a wonderful son and daughter, who have in turn given us a beautiful daughter-in-law and a handsome son-in-law. They have given us three grandsons and a delightful granddaughter. Our family is very close and we honor God, who has truly blessed us all.

When a family lives and works together on a farm, they feel so close to God, nature, and each other. Farming is hard work, long hours, with satisfaction in what you are doing at the end of each day. We never worked on Sunday except for milking the cows. When God's command is "Remember the Sabbath day to keep it holy," we did just that. Our son does the farming now and still keeps this commandment.

Chapter Nine

At the beginning of each year at the Madison School in Adrian, Michigan, we had a class meeting to discuss our class trip, which was the goal we set for the end of the year. We would decide where we would travel, and who would go. They all wanted to go, but they knew it would take money for food, gas, fees, and extras. It was important that the students earn the money and not expect handouts. We only asked for money the first year. They needed to know they could do it themselves and feel proud that they earned their own way.

It was decided that they would earn their traveling money by selling candy, Easter eggs, and doing other projects. Some worked harder than others, so we decided that the ones who worked on a project and sold it had that money credited to their account. We made a large thermometer-type chart that was hung on the wall. Each name was written down in the color of their choice, and credit was added all year. The amount of money we needed for the trip was calculated and divided,

With an average of nine to eleven students and one teacher for ten to fourteen days, I had to have students who were helpers, not problems.

so each knew his or her goal amount. The school secretary kept track of our total money.

It was also decided that not only did they have to work to earn money for the trip, they also had to have good behavior. We could not travel for two weeks together if we had a bad attitude and behavior. With an average of nine to eleven students and one teacher for ten to fourteen days, I had to have students who were helpers, not problems.

Other criteria included class work during the year, which had to be completed to their ability

$\mathscr{A}$ttendance had to be regular.
The children usually were there
unless they were really sick.

level. Attendance had to be regular. The children usually were there unless they were really sick. They enjoyed selling the recipe books; of course, the more books they sold, the more money they could chart. Lots of pillows were made and sold; each also made a pillow for their trip.

There were only three students who had bad behavior or didn't earn their money over all the years; these stayed in the library and had their studies to do. They also forfeited what little they did earn for the class trip. That was a harsh lesson, but a fair one, as everyone was well aware of the rules at the beginning of the year.

Chapter Ten

*E*very student needs to feel successful, and the students I worked with came to my room having failed in the regular classrooms. They were very discouraged and some had an attitude that they were worthless. At first, some felt that they were put in the room for dummies. Many were told repeatedly by their parents and peers that they were "dumb" and "stupid." I would find out what they liked to do, and what their basic skills were, then start them on subjects and projects where they had success and enjoyed the work. It didn't take long before their attitudes and behavior improved and they began to enjoy being in school. I had each one set goals to strive for; it was great to see them achieve these goals. Most went on to graduate and become productive citizens instead of being on welfare, as many of their parents were.

$\mathscr{I}$ decided that I had to somehow teach these special-needs students at their own ability level instead of with the regular classroom textbooks.

I decided that I had to somehow teach these special-needs students at their own ability level instead of with the regular classroom textbooks, which were beyond their ability. It seemed that they were destined to fail in the eyes of the world, but not in my eyes.

When I started teaching special needs, I was in an elementary school room for one year, then a small inadequate room in the high school. Finally, I was given a very nice, large room with a small room attached. The school bought us a heavy-duty Viking sewing machine in a sewing table, and we had a sink, refrigerator, and stove. We really lacked for nothing.

I **was really on my own when it came to making decisions as to what and how to teach my classes.**

I found a series of materials that comprised high school information, but was written at a fifth grade reading level. This series covered history, English, social studies, science, and math. It was perfect for the students.

I was really on my own when it came to making decisions as to what and how to teach my classes. The school board and my principal were cooperative, helpful, and supportive of me, and over the years, their confidence in me grew. I never heard anyone speak out against my ideas; parents and other teachers were always ready to help and support us in every way.

Soon after I began to teach special-needs students, I realized they needed to learn basic life skills. I was always talking with and listening to my students and would hear them say things like, "We don't have a bed at home; we just roll up in a blanket to sleep." Sometimes I would hear them discussing what they had or didn't have to eat at home, such as baloney sandwich or a hot dog for supper. Then I would ask the students, one family at a time, if I could come and visit their mom and dad, and when they would like me to come. It was always a learning experience to meet their parents

𝒥 **always spent time with each student; as they came to know me, they trusted me and would tell me more than they realized.**

and see where and how they lived. I always spent time with each student; as they came to know me, they trusted me and would tell me more than they realized. Making the home calls and seeing how and where they lived told me a lot. Once we became friends, it was easier to help the students help themselves gain confidence and self-worth.

To help them get to know me better, we would take field trips to my farm home each year, and I

$\mathscr{I}$ would take one or two students with me once a month after school to buy groceries.

would have a meal prepared for all to enjoy. They could see the farm and the animals, something many of them had never seen. Then in our study of healthy food and balanced meals, we would learn that we needed to eat meat, vegetables, salads, bread, and drink milk so we would feel good and have energy to work and play.

My next step was to teach the students how to make good, healthy meals. At first, we would make a meal once a week for our group. We would discuss what we would like, then decide which groceries we would buy to make the meal. I often would bring vegetables from the garden, and sometimes the students would want to bring something from their homes. This was a time when we would use math in measuring for a recipe, and reading to be able to know how to follow the steps.

There was quite a bit of preparation for each meal. I would take one or two students with me once a month after school to buy groceries. Here we learned how to shop, compare prices, and work within a budget, as we had only so much money to spend. We also learned that we had to be very

Some students had to be taken to the shower room to take a shower, as personal hygiene was not taught at home.

clean when preparing food. Some students had to be taken to the shower room to take a shower, as personal hygiene was not taught at home. Then near the end of the year, we would plan, prepare, and serve a luncheon to our school staff, who gave the class a donation. It was great fun for our students and delicious for the staff.

Out of this growing knowledge of cooking, the class decided to put together a recipe book, which earned them money for the school trip. This was a big project but turned out to be another great learning experience. The students gathered favorite recipes from their mothers, aunts, and grandmothers and also from the school personnel and friends. Some of the older students wrote letters to the governor's and president's wives who sent theirs and their husbands' favorite recipes. It delighted us to have these "famous" recipes for our book, and probably accounted for most of the sales. We sold over three hundred books in our school district and the students were thrilled. Over twenty-five years' time, my students compiled four recipe books. I

$\mathcal{I}$ found that the students were talented with their hands in many ways.

still run into people who bought our books, and they tell me they are still using and loving the recipes. What a compliment!

I also found that the students were talented with their hands in many ways. I compiled a list of hands-on projects from which the students could choose. Some wanted to make quilts, so we asked teachers and friends to contribute fabric scraps. We learned to measure and use a ruler to make quilt pieces and the result was a beautiful quilt that we raffled off. The class all benefited from the

The Daily Telegram, Friday, May 10, 1985

Madison woman wins quilt

Diane Camp (second from right), president of the Madison Mothers Club, was the winner of a quilt made by members of the special talents class at Madison School. Also pictured are (l-r) stu- dent Bob Schuch, teacher Mrs. Florine Baker, and Gary George, student. Proceeds from the drawing will help finance a class camping trip this spring. (Telegram photo by Roger Hart) experience. The mother who won it spoke to me a few months ago, and is still proud to own it.

Both boys and girls wished to do crochet pieces. One young girl wanted to crochet a shawl, hat, and mittens to match in red, white, and blue. This was a large project, as she had very poor eyesight, but she did finish it. Her eyes had never lost

*T*he only doctor who could do
the operation to fix her eyes
lived in Texas. The Rotary Club
agreed to pay for her to travel.

the covering at birth, and she had only a small area for seeing. She was very pleased with her success. The girl grew to be a fine wife and mother, who kept a clean house. The social worker said she never found any dirty dishes in her sink. I think that this is a great report. At that time, the only doctor who could do the operation to fix her eyes lived in Texas. The Rotary Club agreed to pay for her to travel to Texas, and I said I would go with her, but her parents would not let her go. What a shame. This was hard to understand.

I also had a tall fellow who wanted to crochet a rug. He made a round rug, and one day I saw him lay it on the floor and lie down on it. I asked, "What are you doing?" He said, "I have to make it big enough to sleep on." He had a long way to go, as he was six feet tall, and the rug had to be six feet across. To my surprise, he really did get it done. He had the biggest smile and was so happy. When we left on our class adventure in the spring, he was on his first trip away from home, and when I

I asked if he was okay,
and his big smile and nod of
head told me he was.

looked in the van mirror, he was hugging his pillow. I asked if he was okay, and his big smile and nod of head told me he was.

I also had some students who wanted to learn to upholster, so I took a class in upholstering in order to teach them. One of them brought in a piece of furniture, and we worked together to take off the old fabric. Then we bought some new fabric and ended up with a like-new item to take home. We had an upholstery machine given to us. That made it much easier to upholster chairs and couches for people, and the students learned this great skill and earned money for their trip. They learned to refinish wood furniture, and I was happy to pay them for many items that they refinished for me.

One boy brought in his father's lounge chair to be upholstered. It took a lot of work, but his mother bought the fabric and we worked together until we had it finished. He took it home for his

*O*ne boy brought in his father's lounge chair to be upholstered. It took a lot of work.

father's Christmas present. They were both very happy, the father with his chair and the son for the feeling of great success in a job well done.

In addition to parents and other people assisting us with items to prepare for money, the owner of Merillat Industries contributed financially in our second year; in the years after, he donated cabinet doors by the carload to use for items we could sell. He also gave us cabinets to furnish my classroom with storage space.

We occasionally picked up good, used chairs and other furniture along the streets at spring cleaning time. This was an extra source of trip money, and the students were enthusiastic about making something useful out of castoffs.

Other students wanted to learn to cane chair seats. I had a couple of chairs that needed new seats, so I asked my father to come to school and teach us how to cane. I bought the cane and tools, and several students learned that craft. Some worked in couples, two on a chair. Teachers, friends, and families brought in pieces of furniture to upholster, refinish, or cane; we would charge a fee that would go toward our class trip at the end of the year. This gave them incentive and a goal. Their self-worth was greatly improved as they completed each task.

In the Montana hills.

Chapter Eleven

*E*ach fall we had a project in canning and preserving food. Teachers and friends as well as I, myself, would bring in garden produce such as tomatoes, cucumbers, apples, etc. We canned tomatoes, made relish, apple jelly, and applesauce. We also made green tomato mincemeat. We used some at school in our meals and some we sold to teachers and friends. The students also made pounds and pounds of fudge, which they sold to the students in the elementary, junior high, and high schools. This required counting money and making change without a calculator. I

Michigan trip.

find many people can't do that today. It seems to be a lost art.

At Christmas, we made rock candy and sold bags of it. At Easter, we made sugar eggs and decorated them. People would order them for their

$\mathscr{I}$ soon realized my students all needed to be successful at what they could do.

Easter decorations, and the students earned money and learned a craft as well. I also took a cake decorating class and shared that with the students; some of them went on to decorate cakes for employment.

My Spanish-speaking students were such a happy group. We all wanted to learn how to make tacos, so one of their mothers came to our class and taught us how to make them. Of course, we had no trouble eating them!

I soon realized my students all needed to be successful at what they could do, so I worked at three important things: finding out whatever a child wanted to learn, learning it, and teaching it to them so they could do it well and enjoy the work itself as well as the results. All my students, both boys and girls, could cook and sew; we made no distinctions. Everyone worked on refinishing chairs and furniture. Some were not able to cane well, where others were very good at it. All the projects could help them earn money as adults in employment or for use in their own homes. This

It **is immensely satisfying to see young people learning and succeeding, knowing they can do well and that they have value and self-worth.**

gave them life skills. To me, it is immensely satisfying to see young people learning and succeeding, knowing they can do well and that they have value and self-worth.

As each student reached the age where they could get a job, I would help them and encourage them to do it. I had two boys who began working at McDonald's. They were soon made responsible for opening and closing. I told them to keep busy and always find something to do. Never quit a job until you have another one in your pocket. I found that one of my older students could not write, and he felt very bad about it. I knew that would keep him from finding gainful employment, so I started teaching him, beginning with the first letter of the alphabet. He practiced each small and capital letter and was so proud of himself when he could write well. He said, "Mrs. Baker, no one ever taught me how before." It was so gratifying to see him happy and successful.

Chapter Twelve

I used the interest of the students' trip we planned each year to teach the basics. We started our planning at the beginning of each year and set our goals early. All were interested in taking a learning trip, so we would begin by deciding where we were going: north, south, east, or west. Then I would get material to cover that area. If we decided to go south, then we had all the states from Michigan to Florida to read about. We wrote letters to the Chambers of Commerce of those states, and found out all the historic places of interest to visit. We would divide up the states so that two students worked together on a state. This involved reading, letter writing, and map reading. Then when the mail came, it was very exciting to

We learned directions by observing that the sun always rises in the east, is in the south at noon, and sets in the west at night.

read and share the information with the rest of the class. We learned directions by observing that the sun always rises in the east, is in the south at noon, and sets in the west at night. We also had fun measuring our room to learn yards, feet, and inches. They measured windows, doors, desks, tables, and it was all fun. We really made it a game.

We were going to be cooking on the trip, so they learned to measure with a cup measure, tablespoon, teaspoon, ½ teaspoon, and ¼ teaspoon. They learned how many cups are in a quart or pint, how many quarts in a gallon, etc. I'm amazed at how many adults don't know this information. They did not use a calculator until they knew how to add, subtract, and multiply. They learned multi-plication tables by heart. Today, we have too many people who can't add, subtract, or multiply without a calculator. That's an awful commentary on our school system and our nation.

*𝒯*he first time I took my students on a trip, I realized that most of them needed to learn how people were to live as a family.

The first time I took my students on a trip, I realized that most of them needed to learn how people were to live as a family, with such basics as balanced meals, taking showers, and how to sleep in a bed between sheets. Some of my students were used to rolling up in a blanket and sleeping on the floor or wherever there was space. When we were planning our meals, it was more than a baloney or peanut butter sandwich. We needed meat, vegetables, salad, and dessert. They all took turns helping to plan and cook the meals, do dishes, make beds, and do general cleaning.

Madison special ed students 'hit the road' *May 1989*

Madison High School special education students, members of the "special talents" class, and their teacher, Florine Baker, will spend a lot of time in their van for the next few weeks. They left Thursday for a two-week trip that will take them through Ohio, Indiana, Illinois, Kentucky, Tennessee, Georgia and Florida. Baker calls the van a "classroom on wheels", and says the students will be visiting historical sites along the way, adding that the trip will show the students the places they have studied about all year long. (Telegram photo by Susan Oppat.)

Our first trip was to a cabin on Devil's Lake, only about twenty miles from school. A board member, who had a student in my class, said we could use their cabin for a week, Monday through Friday. We discussed as a group what was needed: clothes, swimsuit and towel, soap, toothbrush, washcloth, pajamas, etc. We had earned enough money for other needs from selling candy, and I furnished the transportation and gas. The school furnished canned goods, and we received a few donations for some extra food. This proved to be a very interesting learning week.

The first day we went to the grocery store, and unknown to me, the boys stole a pack of cigarettes

*T*his gave me a great opportunity to discuss God's commandment, "Thou shalt not steal."

and a couple of cigars. While the girls and I were fixing supper, I looked out the window to check on what the guys were doing and noticed smoke around them. So after supper, when the dishes were done, we gathered for a meeting. I told them what I had seen and asked them where the cigarettes came from. They confessed they had stolen them from the store. This gave me a great opportunity to discuss God's commandment, "Thou shalt not steal." It was the first time some

God is so good and is answering prayer and working miracles today.

of them had heard this commandment from the Bible. So I told them that in the morning, after breakfast, we were going back to the store and tell the owner what they had done. They were very sorry and very afraid he would call the police. They begged me not to take them, and of course the grocer was angry with them and wanted to call the police, but I told him I thought they had learned their lesson. We paid for the smokes and he let us all go. There was such relief in those boys' hearts. One of them is now married with three children and is serving God on the mission field today. God is so good and is answering prayer and working miracles today. We must obey Him and do His will.

*W*e invited our superintendent
for supper. The students
planned and cooked the meal
and entertained him.

On Wednesday of that week, we invited our superintendent for supper. The students planned and cooked the meal and entertained him. They set a proper table and tried to use the silverware correctly. Our guest was impressed and enjoyed his time with us. It was a very good experience.

The second year, our trip was camping in our beautiful state of Michigan. My folks went with us and we used the tent for the boys and my parent's fifth-wheel camper to cook our meals, eat in, and for the girls and me to sleep in. I also drove. We visited many historic places and our travel goal was my cabin on Winslow Lake in the Upper Peninsula. The students loved it. They fished, boated, swam, and enjoyed everything. This took only a small amount of money, as our lodging and

Our group traveled in truck to Florida. The only vehicle we had. I bought a van the next year.

transportation was provided. On subsequent trips, every night we set up a large, divided tent, cooked our food for supper, and went to bed at dark. We always had a Bible story and prayer before going to sleep. The students picked out the stories. Boys slept at one end of the tent, and the girls and I

꙳꙳꙳

*W*e always had a Bible story and prayer before going to sleep.

꙳꙳꙳

slept at the other, near the door. No one got out without my knowing.

When it was time to take my class on their yearly trip, getting a vehicle large enough that we could afford was difficult. The first few years I had a car dealer who lent us a station wagon, and I pulled a trailer for our tents, luggage, and supplies. Then another year, a cousin loaned me his enclosed truck, which held everything. Another year, my dad loaned us his pick-up; we put a camper top on the back, and all but two students rode in the back. Two always rode with me as co-pilots, to read the map and help with directions.

No one ever complained about what we drove. We always had a great time. After that, I bought a van that had no seats, so a board member friend put in seats and charged us nothing. We surely appreciated it. I bought three different vans to use for

$\mathcal{I}$n 1987, the NEA decided that all special-education students should be put back into regular classrooms with regular students and not segregated in rooms like mine.

our trips. It was wonderful when we didn't have to worry about what we were going to drive in.

It is interesting to note that in 1987, the NEA decided that all special-education students should be put back into regular classrooms with regular students and not segregated in rooms like mine. The school board and the superintendent met in my room with the students and me, and they asked the students if they wanted to move to a regular class. They all said no. The parents also supported our teaching methods, which helped the

Class groups.

school board's decision that I continue teaching as I was.

When I retired, the class became a resource room, to comply with state rules. I feel that it is a shame that the young people do not have the same opportunities now that my students had. There are more unhappy, disturbed students now than ever, unable to cope with hard life and disappointments, and lacking the life skills necessary to survive.

What a happy fisherman.

Chapter Thirteen

*T*aking students on these trips took a great deal of planning on my part, as an educator. I expected plenty of learning to be done on the trip, with accountability for what was learned. I include here a basic outline of the learning I expected the students to accomplish:

Maps

I had a book that covered each state and listed information of interest on each. I made copies of each map of the states we were going to travel in and we all learned to read and locate our stops.

Some students became very adept at map reading, but others needed help.

Journals

I bought a notebook and pen for each student before we left. They were expected to keep a journal of the trip. Some wrote interesting stories, but

*W*e compiled the journals
at the end of the trip, and
each student as well as any
school personnel who wanted
one had a copy.

like the map reading, for others keeping a journal was difficult. We compiled the journals at the end of the trip, and each student as well as any school personnel who wanted one had a copy.

Meal Planning

We spent time doing advance meal planning for the entire trip, so the school could allocate food, and so parents could decide what they wanted to contribute. The school gave us gallon cans of vegetables, pudding, fruit, peanut butter, etc. Then every day we consulted our plan and

We would occasionally stop at McDonald's for our lunch of hamburgers, fries, and a coke.

ate accordingly. Some meals at fast-food restaurants were included in our plan, for variety. We would occasionally stop at McDonald's for our lunch of hamburgers, fries, and a coke. It was ninety-nine cents each. They enjoyed that and it saved time.

Often I packed our lunch and we had a picnic at noon when time permitted. We usually bought meat, milk, and eggs before we camped at night. Our breakfast was usually sausage, egg, onion and cheese omelets for breakfast with hot cocoa and bread and jelly until they were full. The favorite suppers were tacos, all they could eat, or goulash with vegetables, bread and butter, pudding, or fruit, and cookies. Most of them gained weight on our trips.

Cooperation and Using Equipment

Tenting was a great experience as we had to learn to work together as a unit or the tent would never get set up and we would not have a place to sleep. Usually, we had a couple of boys who would

$\mathscr{O}$ne night it rained, and we all woke up in wet sleeping bags.

take charge of setting up the tent. They told the others what to do, and it would soon be up. Then the sleeping bags and suitcases were put inside. We never had to set up in the rain, but a few times it stormed at night. One night it rained, and we all woke up in wet sleeping bags. We quickly dressed, packed up the wet tent and went to a laundromat to dry all our bags and wet clothing.

On another trip, one student had a bowel problem in the night, and the boys helped him take his bag to the shower and wash it out. We put it into a plastic bag, and they put it in the van for the trip to a laundromat, where we washed his bag and mine. They had set his bag on top of mine in

A double tent that divided so guys were on one end and girls and I were on door end. It was great but finally fell apart.

the van, and it was drenched, too. Oh, what fun. On one of our last trips, my tent was wearing out.

$\mathcal{I}$ turned on the flashlight and saw that the tent had ripped apart and water was pouring down on her.

That night it rained, and one girl woke up crying, "Mrs. Baker, I'm all wet!" I turned on the flashlight and saw that the tent had ripped apart and water was pouring down on her. It was three A.M. We all got up, packed the tent and everything else into the van, and left to find another laundromat. I think that was the worst night of all our travels.

Health

We found out it was very important to take showers and wear clean underwear every day as we spent lots of time together. We were in close quarters, both in the van and in the tent. The teens found that deodorant was very important. It's a surprise to me that we had only one boy on our first trip get sick. He ate too many dill pickles. Of course, he threw up in the tent and we had a mess to clean up. One boy said, "Golly, Mrs. Baker, it

*P*raying was the spiritual part of our training. We always said a prayer before each meal, at bedtime, and again each morning.

stinks in here!" We all had a good laugh over that statement, and the students learned a lesson about eating in moderation.

Prayer

Praying was the spiritual part of our training. We always said a prayer before each meal, at bedtime, and again each morning before starting our trip or adventure for the day. If I forgot, a student would always remind me by saying, "Mrs. Baker, we didn't have our prayer." I would stop the van and have prayer, then on we would go. Of all the thousands of miles we traveled, we were protected from even one accident. Praise the Lord. We all enjoyed singing as we traveled during the long miles.

Finances and Record Keeping

Each student kept a record of the amount of money they had at the beginning of the trip, what they spent on pop, candy, and gifts during the trip, and what they had left. We had gasoline to buy,

A **student on the trip for the first time might want to buy a pop at each stop, and the money would soon be gone.**

laundromats to stop at, and fees for getting into parks, museums, and many attractions. A student on the trip for the first time might want to buy a pop at each stop, and the money would soon be gone. They soon learned to drink water, which was free, and stretch the money. A few would even have some left over. At the end of each trip, we added up our expenses, gas, food, fees, etc. It was very interesting how much food and gas cost. Each would do the math and then we would compare our answers. We added the miles and number of days, then divided by the number of students.

By the end of the trip, all the students had a real understanding of how much it cost to eat.

They would learn what it cost each day. We always did very well.

Shopping

I always took two or three students shopping for groceries so they could learn how to get the best bargains and also to choose what they liked. By the end of the trip, all the students had a real understanding of how much it cost to eat, how to estimate the amount of food needed, how to budget the money, and how to get the correct change.

Safety

We had only one student whom I had to take to the hospital, and that was when we were at our cabin in the Upper Peninsula. The boys used two boats and went fishing so close together that one boy caught another boy with a fishhook in his eyelid. I was very afraid it was in his eye. I took another student to help, and we rushed to the doctor, who said, "Oh, I have several of these a day." He took out

*O*ne time I had laryngitis, bronchitis, and pneumonia, and I stopped at a clinic for medication.

the hook and gave us a salve to put on it, and the boy didn't need a stitch. God is so good. Of course I always had permission slips from parents for medical help if I needed it. One other time I had laryngitis, bronchitis, and pneumonia, and I stopped at a clinic for medication. We camped for two days at a beach in Florida; the students were a great help to me and still enjoyed swimming and planing. I was soon like new and on we traveled.

Laundry

I instructed each student to pack light, but to be sure to pack fresh pairs of underwear and at

Group at Kentucky horse farm.

least three outfits to last one week. Then we would stop to do laundry, and all had to learn how to put white, colored, and dark clothes in batches to wash. I helped them fold the clothes after they were dry. During one such stop, two of the younger boys decided to block up the toilet. The manager caught them, made them remove all the waste and toilet paper with their hands, and reported to me. It was gross, but they never tried

$\mathscr{I}$t was a time for the students to use their best manners and try food they had never tasted before.

such a thing again. It was a very embarrassing experience for all of us.

Manners

Several times at the end of our tour, we had money enough to eat out at a nice restaurant. Once, I remember well, we went to the Old Fort Restaurant just outside of Mackinaw City. It was a time for the students to use their best manners and try food they had never tasted before. We chose to eat from the food bar; some even tried shrimp and clams. All had a good time and I surely

*E*ach morning a different
student would check the
oil and another would wash
the van windows.

enjoyed not having to cook for one meal. Eleven young people can eat a lot of food.

Auto Maintenance

Each morning a different student would check the oil and another would wash the van windows. We had very few troubles with vehicles. One year when we pulled a trailer behind us, as we turned off the expressway into a small town, the trailer came unhitched. God's protection had us off the expressway when that happened. We found someone to fix it and were on the road again.

The first van I bought had a radiator problem, but again, we found someone to fix it and had a great trip. One year, we had a flat tire, but the boys knew how to fix it. God protected us over thousands of miles over the years. He was so good to us.

Once when we were down in a valley driving through a small town, the kids pointed out that a

*W*e had all been singing happily at the top of our lungs, and I guess I was speeding.

policeman was following us. We had all been singing happily at the top of our lungs, and I guess I was speeding, but he let us off with a warning.

One rule we had for travel was that every time we stopped for gas or at a rest area, everyone used the bathroom. That way we weren't constantly stopping. Once an emergency pit stop was needed, so the fellow made a woods run.

Nature Study

In science, we had studied the planets and some star constellations, such as the Big Dipper, Little Dipper, the Milky Way, and the North Star, and we tried to locate them in the night sky. We also studied wildflowers, trees, and birds, and the students learned to identify them as we traveled. The tamarack tree was one of the most interesting as it looks like a pine but sheds its needles each year and grows new needles in the spring. They learned our state flower, the apple blossom; our state bird, the robin; and our state fish, the brook trout. I really tried very hard to make my lessons well-rounded and to teach all the basic skills they would need to survive in our world, as well as some interesting hobbies to make life more fun.

Chapter Fourteen

$\mathcal{I}$n the classroom, there were difficulties and blessings involved in teaching the upper grades. Many came from single-parent homes, and I felt that some students should be given an A just for showing up each day. They really had to fend for themselves. Some of them had to fix their own food, wash their clothes, and sleep on the floor in a dirty house with a yard full of trash. These young people needed to feel loved and valued. I often would give hugs for a successful job well done. Some needed me to just listen to them and show that I cared. Some had alcoholic parents, some parents were on drugs, and some were chain smokers. I discovered that parents with these types of problems most often had children with learning disabilities. I also had some students from

ℐt was important to teach good study habits and work ethics, as most of my students were not taught these skills at home.

good homes, though, with loving parents who were always supportive and helpful to me.

It was important to teach good study habits and work ethics, as most of my students were not taught these skills at home. There were no duties, jobs, or order around the house. They needed to learn responsibility to family and self as a member of the family group. One girl always came to school dirty. I tried in every way to teach her that she had to bathe and wash every day. Every week or two, I would give her soap, towel, comb, etc., and the counselor, a close friend of mine, would take her to the gym shower and see that she scrubbed clean.

Several students had emotional habits. Some would tap their toes, bite their nails, or just not be able to work. I had carpet laid in my room to counter the tapping and noise. That helped some, so the room was quiet, but it couldn't correct the bad habits.

Some students had problems in thought processing. One boy could not figure out how to do a

*O*ne student had difficulty walking, but he could ride a bike.

problem, but if I would read the problem to him, he knew the answer at once. He could not process it alone. He always tried, but would say, "You read it to me, Mrs. Baker." A dyslexic child or adult also has great difficulty. One student had difficulty walking, but he could ride a bike. He would work very hard and went on our trips, and other students were always kind and helpful to him. After he graduated, he rode his bike to school for visits.

I had one young student who lived with our family most of one year. There were problems at his home, and he always wanted to come home with me, so I would take him. Every time I meet a former student, I thank and praise God for all His many blessings to my very supportive family and me.

Chapter Fifteen

I feel that the training I received in County Normal, at eighteen years of age, and teaching my students at age nineteen in a one-room schoolhouse gave me an educational background as to what young people need in today's world. I taught all grades, kindergarten through eighth, and all subjects, besides keeping a fire in winter and doing janitor work all year. My early home life was such that I knew what hard work and discipline were. My early home life was such that I knew the love of God. We were taught to have a holy fear of doing any wrong and having

God to answer to. The love of God and study of Scriptures gave me a love of everything I put my

I have tried to teach all the young people under my care all the principles needed to live a full and honorable life.

hands to, whether housework, farming, crafts, or teaching.

I have been greatly blessed over the years and have tried to teach all the young people under my care all the principles needed to live a full and honorable life. I've tried to establish an educational and moral foundation in my students' lives that may have been missing in some of their homes. I have had students tell me as they graduated, "You have been more than a teacher; you have been a mom to me." I have always loved my young people. In the end, only what's done for Christ will last forever. We don't own anything; we are just stewards of our possessions and our talents. God gives us what we need; our job is to use what we have to glorify Him.

People are so concerned about their things. When our fifteen-room house in Clinton burned, we were certainly disappointed. After all, we had entertained thousands of people there and had more memories associated with it than we could count. But if God wanted to give it back to us, He

*W*e don't own anything; we are just stewards of our possessions and our talents.

could and He did. When I see people hang onto things or put possessions ahead of friendship, I can't help thinking that I never saw a hearse towing a U-Haul. The only thing we take when we die is our love for Christ and the work we have done in His precious name.

God's Angels with Special Talents
Order Form

Postal orders: 14146 Allen Road
                     Clinton, MI 49239

Telephone orders: 517-456-4228

E-mail orders: BauldyHillFarm@webtv.net

Please send *God's Angels with Special Talents* **to:**

Name: _____

Address: _____

City: _____   State: _____

Zip: _____

Telephone: (_____) _____

Book Price: $16.95

Shipping: $3.00 for the first book and $1.00 for each additional book to
cover shipping and handling within US, Canada, and Mexico.
International orders add $6.00 for the first book and $2.00 for
each additional book.

Or order from:
ACW Press
85334 Lorane Hwy
Eugene, OR 97405

(800) 931-BOOK

or contact your local bookstore